# A Letter to
# Mrs. Roosevelt

# A Letter to Mrs. Roosevelt

## C. COCO DE YOUNG

A Yearling Book

Published by
Dell Yearling
an imprint of
Random House Children's Books
a division of Random House, Inc.
1540 Broadway
New York, New York 10036

Visit us on the Web! www.randomhouse.com/kids

Educators and librarians, for a variety of teaching tools, visit us at www.randomhouse.com/teachers

ISBN 0-440-41529-2

Reprinted by arrangement with Delacorte Press

Printed in the United States of America

August 2000

10  9  8  7  6  5

OPM

*In loving memory of my grandparents,*
*Mike and Carmela Coco*
*and*
*Giuseppe and Giuseppina Camuti*

*To my beloved parents, the believers,*
*Carmel and Mary Kay (Camuti) Coco*

*For my dream keepers,*
*Don, Bryan, CaraMarie, Lauren, and Marisa*

# Chapter 1

## THE SHOOTING STAR
## JOHNSTOWN, PENNSYLVANIA

I never used to pay much attention to the dark. Well, except for the nights when I sat on our front-porch swing, counting the stars and waiting. I would find a patch of stars caught between the rooftops across the street and swing and count, and count and wait.

One night my best friend's mother called to me from her porch next door, "Margo, go inside. It's raining. There are no stars for you to count."

"Thank you, Mrs. Meglio, but I can still see the stars from last night," I called back. I didn't tell her that my eyes were closed tight and I was trying to remember them.

Nighttime was my friend back then, keeping me company while I waited for the trolley car to bring Mama and Papa home. I could hear the clatter as it crossed over the First Street Bridge and turned right onto Maple Avenue. Papa would climb down the steps, then hold out his hand to Mama. I could tell right then if Charlie—he's my little brother—had had a good day or bad.

Charlie had been kicked in the knee when he'd tried to break up a fight between two boys during a game of kickball. He'd convinced Mama and Papa that it was an accident, but I was not so sure. I can remember hearing Charlie groan during the night. I went in to check him, but he was sound asleep. The next morning Charlie's knee looked like a balloon. He stayed in bed all day. It didn't help. When the doctor visited that evening he told Papa to get Charlie to the hospital immediately. The infection in Charlie's knee bone was called osteomyelitis.

Every day for four months Mama and Papa rode the trolley to Mercy Hospital to visit Charlie. Every night for four months I waited for their return.

I was seven. The hospital rules posted in the front lobby said I was too young to visit my brother. That's why I stayed home, although Sister Cecilia did sneak me up to the third-floor children's ward to see Charlie one time. It was in January, right after Charlie's accident. She held her arm out to Mama as if she was guiding her through the halls, and hid me between the folds of the long, draping sleeve of her habit. She told me that two things were certain: if we could get past Mother Superior it would be a miracle, and the best medicine for Charlie was to know how much we all loved him.

Charlie was in a big room with other children, some older and some younger than his five years. I remember rushing over to the pillow covered with the familiar dark brown curls. "Charlie," I whispered, "I've come to take you home." I would help Mama and Papa take care of Charlie.

Charlie opened his eyes, and my heart sank at the same time. He looked all swallowed up in that big hospital bed with sides like a crib. I knew then that it would be a long time before Charlie would play Caddy with me and my best friend, Rosa. I just knew I would have to wait to play anything with Charlie, and I did.

Nobody ever told me why Sister Cecilia snuck me up to his room, but I think they were afraid Charlie would die. He was sick, really sick. The doctor operated on Charlie's knee, but the infection spread further down. The doctor wanted to amputate Charlie's leg above the knee. Papa told the doctor he would do anything he had to do to save Charlie's leg—the whole leg. That was when he and Mama found out about the doctor in Boston—if he couldn't help Charlie, then nobody could. Papa arranged for him to come to Johnstown and operate on Charlie's leg. Charlie ended up with a stiff knee, and he wore a shoe with a raised heel, but the doctor saved Charlie's whole leg.

Charlie finally came home at the end of April. At night he sat on the porch swing with me. He would point to the different constellations; then I would count the stars in them. We could hear Mama humming inside, and we thought the worst was over. It wasn't.

~~~

Everything started to change in May, after Mrs. DiLuso saw the shooting star. I remember she didn't even knock. I had just mopped the parlor floor for Mama when Mrs. DiLuso came rushing through the front door. With one step onto the wet floor, that four-foot-high, four-foot-around woman was all arms and legs, screeching wildly, "Oh, aaah, Ma-a-a-ma mia!" as she slid across the room.

One look from Mama and I bit the sides of my cheeks to keep from laughing at Mrs. DiLuso, the human cannonball. I stayed in the room long enough to see her come to a crashing halt, sprawled across the small table where I had sorted my postcard collection. Later Mama explained that Mrs. DiLuso had seen a star shooting across the sky above our neighborhood the night before. According to Mrs. DiLuso, who is very superstitious, it meant death or bad times for someone on Maple Avenue. There must have been a lot of shooting stars that night.

That same week Miss Penton, my teacher at Maple Avenue School, decided to fail the entire second grade. She insisted that there were students in our class who were not ready for third grade. If she failed one, she promised, she would fail everyone . . . and she did.

My papa was the only parent who wasn't afraid of Miss Penton's sharp tongue and puckered lips. He walked me to school one morning after the announcement, then made me wait in the hallway while he spoke with her. I heard him introduce himself. I didn't hear a word from Miss Penton. Papa went on to explain that he and Mama felt certain that I was prepared to attend third grade next year. He told her that I could add, subtract, multiply, use a cash register, make change, and write orders at our family store. I knew Miss Penton was angry; I heard her tapping a ruler on her desk the way she always did when someone crossed her. Miss Penton either ignored Papa's explanation, or did not hear a word he said while she tapped away. She simply told Papa that we Italian immigrants were in America now, and that our last name, Bandini, should be changed to Bandin. I couldn't hear what Papa said to Miss Penton, but my full name, Margo Bandini, remained on my report card. Papa won one battle, and Miss Penton won the other. The entire class, including Rosa and me, repeated the second grade.

That was four years ago, in 1929. Everything has changed on Maple Avenue. And to think I wasn't afraid—not then.

# Chapter 2

## MAPLE AVENUE, 1933

Papa owned a shoe repair shop on Bedford Street. I often walked to work with him when there was no school. Every morning at six o'clock he crossed over the First Street Bridge, stopped to greet Mr. Bobb, who operated the train tower on the bridge, then walked the long trek past the steel mill. Papa stopped whistling and tipped his hat in respect as he passed St. John's Church. At the corner near the Swank Building, he started to whistle again, and continued until he reached the shop. As Papa unlocked the door he would pause to breathe in the balmy scents of leather and shoe polish. Then he'd turn on the lights, walk behind the counter, and put on his apron.

In the late afternoon, Papa closed the shop and walked past the bank on Main Street. There was a time when he would stop in the bank every Friday, just before closing. That was when he carried a small sack of money, proof of a busy week. He would smile as he proudly handed the sack over to the teller behind the counter. Sometimes Mr. Lockhard, the bank president, would smile back and shake Papa's hand. Not anymore. Now Papa walked by the bank jingling the small change in his pocket, sometimes carrying a basket of fresh fruit and vegetables.

Today I heard him tell Mama that Mr. Lockhard stood in the window of the bank yesterday. Papa tipped his hat, but Mr. Lockhard didn't seem to notice as he stared out at Main Street. He stopped shaking Papa's hand a long time ago, when Papa stopped carrying the money sack. Now Papa used the pocket change to pay our food bill.

Mr. Frappa, who owned a grocery store on Maple Avenue, kept a large black ledger of all the money people owed him. Every Friday Papa handed me our account book and sent me across the street to Mr. Frappa's store.

I knew we weren't poor. We had our house, a radio, and food. Rosa lived next door in her house. Her father was a steelworker.

One family in our neighborhood had to move away, one cold March day. It happened after the sheriff posted a sign on their front door—SHERIFF SALE, in big black letters. They had to leave everything behind except for the suitcases they carried, the clothes they wore, and their cat. I didn't tell Mama, but Rosa and I peeked into their basement window last week. It gave me the shivers to see their towels still hanging on the clothesline and the cat's box next to the stairs. Nobody knew where they went.

Mrs. DiLuso visited Mama tonight. Her visit seemed to carry a cloud of icy gloom, even though it was the middle of April. Cold chills ran down my spine as she reminded Mama that *il diavolo*, the devil, had brought the Depression to Maple Avenue the night she saw the shooting star. My fifth-grade teacher, Miss Dobson, said the Great Depression started in October of 1929, when the stock market crashed, banks closed, and people lost their money and their jobs. She even told us about wealthy men who had jumped out of windows because they had lost everything they owned.

Maple Avenue was snuggled between twin hillsides. There were no wealthy people or fancy houses in my neighborhood. Our house was painted brown and had three stories. My bedroom was directly above our front porch and had two huge windows that met in the corner. From the front window I could see all of Maple Avenue, from the brickyard to the Acme Bakery. The side window looked out onto Rosa's front porch and, beyond that, St. Anthony's Church.

Tonight I could hear the steady squeak of the

front-porch swing as it rocked Mama and Papa back and forth. They often sat there at night while they talked.

"Margo, time for bed," called Mama.

"Good night, Mama and Papa."

I would leave the windows open. I didn't mind if the breeze came in, so long as the dark stayed out.

# Chapter 3

~~~

## MAPLE AVENUE NEWS

"Little brothers can be such a nuisance," announced Rosa.

I glanced back at Charlie and Rosa's younger brother, Michael.

"I heard that," Charlie yelled back.

"Well, then hurry," I called over my shoulder. "If the bell rings before we get to school, we'll all be staying after school, on a Friday afternoon."

The boys were walking a half block behind us. Charlie was showing Michael the gold pocket watch Papa had let him take to school today.

"I should remind you that Charlie is only one grade behind us," I told Rosa.

"I might remind *you* that as long as they're both wearing knickers and not long pants, they're still our little brothers," chided Rosa. "Where did he get that watch, anyway?"

"Papa was given that watch after the Great War. It belonged to a friend of his, a soldier Papa knew in the Yankee Division of the United States Army. They were stationed in France together. Papa received his United States citizenship papers while he was on the battlefield in the war. His friend died on that same battlefield. I'm not certain which Charlie is more fascinated by, the story behind the watch or the watch itself." I glanced over at Rosa, who came to a dead halt and stood there shaking her head.

"Your father let Charlie take something that valuable to school?"

I had to admit, even I was surprised. Papa kept that watch in the drawer of the server with his medal and his citizenship papers. Charlie was allowed to look at it, but Papa had never allowed him to take it out of the house before today.

"Maybe Papa thinks Charlie is growing up, even if he is in knickers." Teasing Rosa was something I loved to do. She was always so serious.

We made it to our seats as the bell rang. At lunchtime I saw Charlie showing the watch to a group of boys from my class. I started to wonder what Charlie had told everybody about the pocket watch. He was surrounded by fifth-grade girls at dismissal and didn't look the least bit shy about it.

"Catch me," I shouted as I tagged Rosa on the way home. It felt good to know the weekend was here.

Mama must have agreed, because Rosa and I sat and talked on my front porch until Papa came home for dinner. I didn't have to set the table or peel potatoes.

"Margo, take this to Mr. Frappa, please." Papa opened the screen door and handed me the account book, a dollar bill, and some change. "Call Charlie to dinner on your way home."

Charlie. Come to think of it, I hadn't seen him since we'd left school.

"He's probably at my house," answered Rosa. "I'll send him along. I have to go home for dinner, too."

I ran across the street to the grocery market. The bell on the door jingled as I walked in. Mr. Frappa was talking to Mrs. DiLuso and another customer. I walked over to the candy counter to wait my turn. My mouth watered, just looking at the peanut butter kisses and roasted peanuts.

"Gypsies . . . ," I could hear Mrs. DiLuso whisper, ". . . near Grandview Cemetery . . . the wealthy . . . steal food . . ."

The Gypsies had come to Johnstown before. Anything and everything that had been lost or stolen was blamed on their arrival. They were back, and so were the rumors. I put my nose up against the glass of the candy counter. I was sure that sweet smell was coming from the peanut butter kisses.

Mr. Frappa's grocery store had one of the few telephones in the neighborhood, and a radio, too. He always seemed to get the news first, then shared it with anyone who was interested. Mrs. DiLuso was always interested. She preferred to report her own version of the news to the neighborhood.

"Steal children . . . ," added the other customer.

Mr. Frappa smiled at me. He knew better than to interrupt and open his ledger while Mrs. DiLuso was there. I glanced up at the price board behind him.

Pork Chops, pound...........................15¢
Large Egg Plants........................2 for 15¢
U.S. No. 1 Potatoes ...................Bushel 75¢
5 Lb. Sack Pastry Flour........................9¢
Iceberg Lettuce, head ..........................5¢
Fancy Sweet Peppers, each.....................1¢
Cocoanut Cup Cakes .....................4 for 5¢
Peanut Butter Kisses, pound ..................10¢

Mmmm, I could get a whole lot of peanut butter kisses for ten cents. I tried to think of something else. It was getting harder to wait for Mr. Frappa. I walked back to the door and looked for Charlie. I sure hoped he'd remembered to return Papa's watch before he'd gone out to play.

"*Scusi*, excuse me." Mrs. DiLuso was standing behind me.

I moved to let her and the other customer out the door.

"Ah, Margo. It's good to see you." Mr. Frappa was at my side.

I handed Mr. Frappa the money and our account book. He walked to the back of the counter and opened the ledger to our name. The page was filled with numbers. He counted the money I gave him, wrote the amount in his book and ours, then subtracted. We still owed him $12.75.

"Thank your mama and papa for me, Margo." He closed the books. "What news do you bring me today?"

I had to smile. The fun was about to begin. Miss Dobson's father owned the local newspaper. She'd bring the daily edition to school every morning and use the first ten minutes of geography class to discuss the news. Mr. Frappa and I enjoyed a good game of news tag at least once a week.

"Miss Dobson told us today that the drought in Oklahoma is so bad, the topsoil blows away in the wind." I was proud of myself. Mr. Frappa had been a teacher somewhere near Pittsburgh. He'd returned to Johnstown to tend the family store after his school was closed down because they couldn't pay the teachers.

"Did you know that entire families are leaving their Oklahoma farms and moving west to find work in California? They call them Okies," he told me. Mr. Frappa always got the last word in.

Last year he used the price board as a news board to keep track of Amelia Earhart's flight across the Atlantic, to inform his customers that the New York Yankees had won the World Series, and to let them know that Franklin Delano Roosevelt had beaten Herbert Hoover in the presidential election. Sometimes his store felt like a classroom. He always made the neighborhood children count their own change. He even gave me a postcard for my collection. It had a picture of the Empire State Building on it, the world's tallest building.

"Charlie was in today. He—"

"Charlie! Dinner! Oh boy, I'm in trouble." I shouted a good-bye to Mr. Frappa as I ran out the door and headed home. *Please, Charlie, be home.* When I got back to the house, Mama and Papa were waiting at the dinner table.

"Come, Margo. Dinner is getting cold. Charlie should be along soon," said Mama.

I was relieved that they didn't ask me if I'd looked for him. It took him a little longer to get around, and he often arrived home just as we sat down to dinner.

But Charlie had really done it this time. Mama never said a word all through dinner, and kept glancing at the door. Papa asked me about my school day, but I could tell by the way he kept looking at Mama that he was wondering about Charlie, too.

"Margo, you wash the dishes, and I will clear the table," said Mama as we finished eating.

I knew it was not the right time to share my thoughts about the unfairness of it all. Charlie had missed dinner, and now Mama was doing his job.

I finished washing the dishes and turned to see Papa standing at our front door. "Margo, where did you go to look for Charlie?"

I remembered our account book in my pocket and handed it to him. "Papa, I was talking to Mr. Frappa and didn't have time to look for Charlie. Maybe Rosa forgot to tell him to come home, too." The troubled look in Papa's eyes made me add, "I'm sure he took very good care of your pocket watch, Papa." I opened the drawer to pull out the watch as proof. The watch wasn't there. I didn't even stop to close the drawer.

"Papa, I'll go find Charlie," I called. The screen door slammed shut behind me. Maybe Rosa was right—little brothers in knickers were a nuisance. Charlie was in trouble for not returning the watch when he got home from school, and now I was in trouble for not finding him.

# Chapter 4

## CHARLIE

Rosa's front door was closed. I knocked hard. No answer. I could hear shouting inside. That seemed to happen often at Rosa's house. I knocked harder. Rosa came to the front door, opened it wide enough to squeeze through, and closed it behind her. She had been crying.

"Are you okay, Rosa?"

She looked at me and swallowed hard. "The steel mill cut my father's work hours again. He's working one day a week now. My mother insists on taking in sewing and laundry. I could help, too. But my father won't let us. He believes it's a man's job to support his family, and that if my mother and I have to work, then he has failed us all. He wants us to move to Buffalo, New York. He heard there's work there for any man who wants it."

"Oh, Rosa, you wouldn't kid me, would you?

We've been friends all our lives." I tried to keep my voice steady and to act grown up. But the thought of my best friend moving away made me feel like a lost little kid.

"My father said he won't wait for the sheriff to post a sign on our door. He said we'll leave before anybody comes to force us out. We don't have the money to pay our mortgage."

A loud crash from inside quieted both of us. Michael came running down the narrow sidewalk that led from their backyard. He suddenly looked much younger than nine. His beet-red face was smudged with grime and streaks of tears.

His voice cracked. "I—I had to do something to stop the shouting. I won't move to Buffalo."

Rosa looked through the window of the front door. Her mother was picking up the scattered pieces of a glass vase.

"Michael, I think you'd better stay with us for a while. We can sit on Margo's front porch." Rosa looked at me the same way she did when I had that rare licorice whip and was debating whether or not I should share it.

"I'm not so sure you want to do that," I said. "I'm in just as much trouble as you are. Michael, if Charlie isn't with you, then where is he? He never came home for dinner."

"I haven't seen him since, uh, since after school."

Mama had a way of knowing when I wasn't telling the truth. All she had to say was, "Margo, your chin is growing." It worked every time. There was something in the way Michael rolled his big blue eyes and bit his lower lip that made me suspect he knew more than he was telling. But I couldn't wait any longer. If Papa didn't have the pocket watch back soon, Charlie and I would both be punished.

"Look, if you see Charlie, tell him he'd better get home fast with Papa's watch."

"Sorry, Margo." Rosa pulled Michael to her side. "We'd come with you to look for Charlie, but . . ."

"It's okay." Something deep inside me stirred. I remembered what it was like to want to protect a little brother. I turned away just in time to see Mrs. DiLuso walking up the steps of my front porch. For once I was thankful for her timing. She would occupy Mama and Papa while I found my little brother.

Charlie was an altar server at St. Anthony's Church, and had become friendly with some of the boys who lived at the church's orphanage. I walked to the back of the orphanage where a group of boys were playing kickball. Charlie wasn't there, and nobody had seen him all day.

I ran to the coal heap. It was nothing more than a fenced-in piece of land where workmen poured the used coal ashes from the brickyard ovens. Charlie often took a small tin bucket there, to collect the chunks of coal left in the pile. Mama was so angry with him the first time he came home covered in black that she made him promise to deliver anything he found to the family with the cat. That was before the SHERIFF SALE sign went up and they were forced to leave their home. I wondered if Mama knew that, since they'd moved, Charlie traded the coal chunks for pieces of candy at Frappa's. I swore that if Charlie didn't show up soon, I'd tell Mama myself.

A horn beeped outside a neighbor's house across the street. A group of kids deserted a game of dodgeball in the alley to examine the shiny black car. I crossed the street to see if Charlie was with them. One of the kids said he'd seen Charlie in Frappa's Grocery Store after school. That was all anybody knew.

I turned and ran back down the street. The sun was setting when I got to Frappa's. The store was dark and the door was locked. I wished I had listened more closely when Mr. Frappa had mentioned he'd seen Charlie. I ran to the brickyard.

The corner lot between the factory and the neighborhood houses supported an elevated train track. A tunnel under the tracks led from the lot into another open area. Rosa had seen the older boys smoking in there last week. I called through the tunnel, "Cha-ar-lie. Charlie, you answer me right now." But there was no answer.

I couldn't help feeling that this was not good. My stomach flip-flopped as my mind raced back in time. The last time Charlie had missed dinner was the evening Mama and Papa rushed him to the hospital. I shook my head and tried to erase the terrible memory. I stomped my foot and let out a groan that echoed through the tunnel, then turned and looked up Maple Avenue one last time as I headed toward home.

Everybody on Maple Avenue knew Charlie. He'd stop a game of kickball to help carry a neighbor's groceries, then turn around and get into mischief in the wink of an eye. Mr. Bobb had to chase him off the arches of the bridge one day. Charlie and Michael had wanted to see who could climb the highest without getting caught. There was quite an uproar the day Charlie snuck a garter snake into school. The principal pulled me out of Miss Dobson's class and made me walk Charlie home.

Here I was again. When Charlie got into mischief, I got into trouble. It was a good thing Charlie wasn't a twin. Lola Nola, a girl in my class, had too many brothers, including a set of twins. Everybody called them Double and Trouble. Lola came to school one time with a fat lip. She had been punished for not watching her younger brother. He was caught stealing apples from . . . Stealing? *Stealing?*

I stopped dead in my tracks. "Stealing?" I said

out loud. My mind raced back in time again, to Mr. Frappa's store and to what I had heard. What had the customer said about the Gypsies stealing children? Mrs. DiLuso would know, and I knew where to find her.

# Chapter 5

## THE SEARCH

By the time I got home, my heart felt as if it would pop right out of my chest. Papa met me at the front door.

The words were caught in the back of my throat. I was afraid to hear myself say them. "I—I can't find him, Papa. Nobody has seen Charlie since Mr. Frappa's store. He was there after school, then left."

I glanced at Mrs. DiLuso, who was shaking her head and beating at her chest with a clenched fist. "*Il diavolo*, again. The Gypsies have your Charlie." "*Stai zitto*, keep quiet!" Papa's dark brown eyes were like daggers. Dead silence followed.

My papa never talked to Mama like that. People loved my papa. He helped everyone. The farmers always went into the shoe shop to see Papa. He would fix their shoes even if they didn't have money. They would trade a basket of fruit and vegetables for a pair of heels. Papa would bring the basket home, and what Mama didn't use we gave to the neighbors. Everybody loved my papa. He never talked like that to anyone.

Mama's eyes filled with tears. I wasn't sure if she was embarrassed by Papa's outburst, or if she believed Mrs. DiLuso.

"Margo, think hard," said Papa in a much gentler tone. "Why would Charlie not come home? Where could he be?"

"It's your watch, Papa. He didn't return it to the drawer. He had it when I saw him, but that was on our way home from school. Papa, what if one of the Gypsies saw Charlie with the gold watch? Charlie would never let anyone take it away from him. He knows what that watch means to you. What if the Gypsies took Charlie and the watch? They steal chickens and *children*—everybody knows that." I looked at Mrs. DiLuso, certain she would agree. Her head was down and her eyes were closed. Was she praying, or was she expecting Papa to yell again?

"I heard those rumors in the shop today," said Papa. "Officer Franks stopped in to pick up his shoes. The only report of anything missing is a crate of chickens that fell off the back of a farmer's truck on his way in from Somerset County."

Mrs. DiLuso looked straight at Papa. "Aaah, so

we still have missing chickens, a missing boy, and now a missing watch. Three. Bad luck comes in threes."

Papa's hands were clenched at his sides. He looked at Mama, shook his head, and said, "I will find Charlie." He was out the front door before we could say another word.

I caught up with Papa as he knocked on Rosa's door and asked for her father. Mr. Meglio helped Papa round up the other neighbors, and they went looking for my brother. Rosa was at my side. Maple Avenue echoed with shouts of "Charlie! Charlie Bandini!"

It looked like a neighborhood game of hide-and-seek, with everybody searching and calling his name. Charlie was the best at hiding. I just hoped he'd shout "Base!" real soon. It was getting dark.

# Chapter 6

~~~

## UNDER THE BRIDGE

This time Rosa helped me search all the areas of Maple Avenue where Charlie played. As before, nobody had seen him. We went to the loading dock at the Acme Bakery. The boys sometimes went there at closing. The damaged goods were left in a bin for the hoboes getting off trains near the brickyard. Charlie was not permitted on the dock. Just last week Rosa and I had caught Michael and Charlie eating crushed cinnamon rolls in an alley next to the bakery. If I hadn't been so worried, I'd have stopped looking, to tell Mama and Papa that story, too. Maybe, just maybe I would.

The search continued in the field and parking lot behind St. Anthony's. It was getting too difficult to see anyone or anything. I felt better with Rosa at my side. We joined the search in the alleyway behind my house. Lining the alley on the other side was a row of empty lots. It suddenly dawned on me that nobody had checked along the steep bank of the river, past the lots. Charlie was not permitted there, either. The river's strong current would suck in a kid like milk in a straw. I walked to the edge of the lots and looked down. I squinted and tried to see beyond the dark shadows of the steep bank.

"Rosa, I think I know where Charlie might be." My voice remained calm, but fear rushed through me, moving as swiftly as the water I heard below.

"I'm not allowed down there and neither are you, Margo. It's too dangerous. What if you lose your footing and fall in the river?"

"Rosa, you're always asking 'what if.' Well, here's a 'what if' for you. What if my brother lost his footing and is lying down there all alone?" No sooner were the words out of my mouth than I knew I had hurt Rosa's feelings. I watched her run back to the dark alley.

I closed my eyes. The darkness was all around me. I could feel it touching my skin. I knew that if I waited much longer it would cover Charlie like a blanket.

*"The only thing we have to fear is fear itself."* I could remember the picture of President and Mrs. Roosevelt in the newspaper Miss Dobson had brought to school. Those were the very words Franklin Delano Roosevelt had said on the day of his inauguration.

*The only thing we have to fear is fear itself.* I could picture the words printed across Mr. Frappa's board. Under it he had written *FDR, March 4, 1933.* Mr. Frappa told all us kids to remember those words and to use them wisely. He said they might come in handy someday.

"Someday" had come for me. It was here and now.

I opened my eyes and looked into the endless dark. I could see the silhouette of the bridge. Under it was the glow of a small fire.

I started down the steep bank. I didn't want to think about the weeds reaching up like prickly fingers around my knees. I focused my attention on the small fire. The crickets seemed to call out, "Go back, go back." I stopped. I should never have yelled at Rosa. She would know what to do.

I could hear the water; the edge of the river must be very close. I decided to stay farther up along the bank and continue toward the bridge. My feet kept sliding on the weeds and rocks. Stones broke loose under my feet and rolled down the bank into the water. Beads of sweat rolled down my forehead and into my eyes. I wondered if President Roosevelt had ever gone hunting for a little brother in the pitch black.

"Charlie! Charlie! Come on, Charlie! I know you're under there." I was a stone's throw from the bridge. I could see the small campfire clearly.

"Everybody's looking for you. Papa won't be mad about the watch, he just wants you home." I edged closer. I could smell something cooking, in a tin can sitting in the flames.

"He ain't here, missy." I heard a gruff voice and caught a glimpse of a tall, bearded man standing in the shadow of the fire.

"Gypsies!" I screamed at the top of my lungs, and ran.

The bank of the river was steeper than I had realized. My hands and legs were bloody and bruised as I stumbled on the rocks and grabbed at the weeds, pulling myself up the steep slope. I could hear someone running. He was behind me, chasing me, reaching out to grab me. Was this what he'd done to Charlie? A loud scream rang in my ears. My scream. An arm reached out and pulled me to the top of the bank.

"Papa, I—" Everything went blank as I collapsed into his arms.

# Chapter 7

## THE POCKET WATCH

I could hear Mama's voice calling me. "Margo. Margo. Wake up, Margo."

I opened my eyes to a roomful of people staring down at me. I was on the parlor couch and Papa was kneeling at my side. Mama patted a cool, damp cloth against my forehead.

I sat up so fast, the cloth in Mama's hand went flying.

"Papa, I know the Gypsies have Charlie!" I blurted out. "A man was chasing me, trying to take me away, too."

"Margo, calm down. That man was only trying to reach you to hold on to you. He was afraid you'd fall and land in the river. Now, your Mama and I are grateful for his help, and you need to thank him." Papa ran his hand through his dark, wavy hair and stood up. His height and his stern voice made me feel small and silly for what I'd thought and said.

A bearded man stood inside our front door shifting his weight from foot to foot, as though he was afraid to move. He held his cap in one hand and waved to me with the other. Papa called him over.

"Missy," the stranger said in the same gruff voice I'd heard earlier, "you sure did give me a fright. I think you scared me as much as I scared you. I thought for sure you'd fall back into that river. I ain't never seen nobody climb a riverbank that fast. I wasn't chasin' you, I was trying to catch you. But I ain't seen your Charlie, and I sure ain't seen no Gypsies. I been under that bridge for two days, waitin' to catch the eastbound train. I hear there might be work in the apple orchards in New York State. I sure am sorry if I scared you, missy."

A deep groan escaped from my lips. I closed my eyes as tightly as I could. I could feel the heat rising inside me. I felt like such a fool. It was useless to try and hide my beet-red, burning ears. Like the flashing red light on the train tower, my ears were a signal to everybody, letting them know just how embarrassed I was.

I looked up at the man standing next to Papa. His eyes locked with mine, and in that split second it felt as if I could see straight into his heart. I wondered if Charlie, wherever he might be, was feeling like this man. Lonely.

"I'm sorry, too," I said. "I should never have gone down there in the dark. Thanks for your help."

"You should also thank Rosa. She came to get me." Papa turned to Mama and added, "We've searched everywhere for Charlie."

I suddenly felt very tired. I looked at Mama. Her chestnut-brown hair had been neatly pulled back in a chignon earlier today. Now strands of hair had escaped the pins and were hanging in curls around her face and neck. Her brown eyes had lost their usual twinkle and looked like dark, empty pools. People always told me I looked exactly like my mother—I wondered if I looked like her right now.

"Rosa, please help Margo upstairs." Mama looked at Mrs. Meglio, who nodded in agreement.

"Rosa, I'm sorry about what I said earlier," I whispered as we climbed the steps to the second floor. "If I had listened to you, they might have found Charlie by now and not wasted time on me."

I turned to look at Mama one last time. She usually blew Charlie and me a kiss from the bottom step when we went to bed. Instead she was standing at the front door, handing the man with the beard a loaf of bread she had baked yesterday. It was the first time a hobo had ever come to our front door. They always came to the back door.

"He would have scared me too, Margo." Rosa always seemed to be able to read my mind.

"Papa always says the hoboes like to work for the food given them. I hope Mama gave him some fruit with that loaf of bread. He sure did earn it."

Rosa went into my bedroom while I washed up in the bathroom. When I returned to my room, she was sitting as straight as a rod on my bed. She put a finger to her lips, motioning me to be quiet. With the other hand she pointed to the floor under my bed. I stood still.

We could hear a slow, deep vibrating snore in, and a soft, steady, long breath out. There is only one person I know who can fall asleep just about anywhere and snore his way through anything. I knelt down next to my bed and yanked Rosa to her knees. Together we lifted the skirt of the bedspread, and together we shouted, "Charlie Bandini!"

A herd of feet came running up the stairs. Papa was the first one into my room and down on his knees. He pulled my brother out from under the bed and onto his feet.

"What's all the racket for?" Charlie looked at Mama and all the people standing in my room. He was rubbing his eyes as though a good night's sleep had been stolen from him.

Papa hugged Charlie tightly, then shook him. Then he hugged him again as if to make certain it was really Charlie.

Amid all the chatter and confusion Charlie leaned over and asked me, "What took you so long?"

I just shook my head and stared, and then there it was again—like the flashing red light on the train tower. But this time it was Charlie's ears that were burning. He looked at all the faces staring at him and then broke the silence.

"Papa and Mama, I'm sorry. I heard everybody calling me but I knew I'd be in trouble, so I was hiding up here, waiting for Margo. I thought she'd help me, but she never came up. I guess I fell asleep."

Mama pulled Charlie to her side. "In trouble for what, Charlie? Help you with what, Charlie?"

Charlie knelt down on his good knee and reached under the bed. "This," he said as he pulled out a small box. It was filled with tiny golden pieces spread from edge to edge. In the middle of the box was the case of Papa's gold watch, opened and empty.

"I dropped it on the sidewalk when Michael and I were walking home from school. It stopped working, Papa." The burning redness of Charlie's ears spread across his face. His eyes brimmed with tears. "I borrowed a tiny screwdriver from Mr. Frappa. I—I thought I could f-fix it."

# Chapter 8

## THE LADY

I woke to the clanging bell of the trolley car going down Maple Avenue. Saturday was well under way by the time I kissed Mama good morning. She had already been to Frappa's store to buy lard, and had gone to the farmer's truck in the alley behind St. Anthony's Church. The farmer and his wife came once a week to sell fresh eggs, butter, and produce. I often went with Mama to help her carry everything. But today it was a relief to know I wouldn't have to face the neighborhood first thing in the morning.

Saturday was usually the day Charlie spent with his pal Frankie from the orphanage. Frankie was one of the older boys and was often sent on errands in town. Charlie would go with him, and the nuns would give Frankie some extra free time. He and Charlie liked to spend it at the bridge helping Mr.

Bobb operate the gate when the trains passed by. I saw Frankie headed into town by himself this morning.

Late last night, after everybody had left our house, Mama and Papa talked to Charlie and me. They decided Charlie would go to work with Papa every Saturday. I wasn't sure if that was meant to be a punishment for Charlie. He already had his own shoeshine kit and shoe stand in Papa's shop, and could rip the old heels and soles off the steel-workers' boots.

Mama and Papa were more relieved than angry about last night's ordeal. But they did let Charlie and me know that we had to be more responsible.

Papa told me I was lucky to have learned such a valuable lesson at a young age. "Margo, rumors are dangerous. They are like weeds in a garden. If they are not stopped, they will grow and grow until they choke out everything else. Our neighbors were scared last night. They might have gotten angry, too. What if they had listened to you and gone after some Gypsies, or after that hobo?"

I knew my ears were burning red again. I could only think, *Better my ears than my behind.* Somehow Lola Nola came to mind. I had heard that her father used a belt to teach a lesson. I wondered if that was a rumor, too. Rumor or not, Papa's stern words did not feel so harsh after all.

The day passed by quickly. Rosa came over. We

sat in my room sorting through the postcards. The newest addition to my collection was the card Mr. Frappa had given me. I stared at it and wondered if I would ever get to see the Empire State Building.

We made up stories about the pictures. Most of the postcards were old and had been sent to Mama and Papa before the Depression. Now our friends and relatives spent the little money they had on food and bills. Nobody we knew traveled very far—not anymore.

When we grew tired of the postcards, we pretended that we were "Eleanor Everywhere," the President's wife, visiting faraway places. Miss Dobson had told us she earned that nickname because she traveled everywhere for President Roosevelt. She had become his "eyes and ears" ever since he had been struck with polio. Eleanor Roosevelt visited people and places all across the country to see how they were doing, then took the information back to the President. He decided how to help them. Rosa and I hoped Eleanor Roosevelt would come to Johnstown someday. Maybe she could help the people who worked in the steel mills. Then Rosa wouldn't have to move.

Rosa was carrying on, pretending she was Eleanor Everywhere speaking at the Chicago World's Fair.

The sound of a far-off train whistle caught my attention. "Shhh, Rosa, it's coming."

We had just enough time to tuck the postcard collection away in the trunk under my window. We closed the heavy lid and scrambled onto its top. I opened the window facing Maple Avenue and pulled Rosa to my side.

"Okay," said Rosa, "I say seven cars and the lady is seated in the middle of the fourth car wearing her gray hat."

I elbowed Rosa and said, "There are always seven cars, and she always wears her gray hat, and she always sits in the middle of the fourth car *when* she's on the train."

Rosa and I waited for the Saturday-night excursion train every week. It took people from Johnstown to New York City. A second whistle echoed between the twin hillsides. I could hear the slow, steady *clickety-clack, clickety-clack* as the train snaked its way through town.

Rosa shouted, "There it is!" just as the train appeared on the trestle near the brickyard. The lights stayed on in the passenger cars, and the train would not gain speed until it passed the Acme Bakery. We had just enough time to catch a glimpse of the passengers.

Together we counted, "Engine, one, two, three, four—there she is!" The lady with the gray hat was on the train every other Saturday. We couldn't see her face. She had light-colored hair, and she always tilted her gray hat in such a way that we couldn't even see her profile.

"Well, I think she's off to see a Broadway show. She will then meet a wealthy man, get married, and never come back," I said.

"You silly." Rosa laughed. "If she can afford to go on that train, then she already *is* wealthy."

"Okay," I said, "then she's a spy and has her hat pulled down so we can't see who she is."

"I don't think a spy would be all dressed up and headed out of town on an excursion train twice a month," said Rosa.

The train whistle sounded one last time as it picked up speed and disappeared into the darkness.

I knew our game of make-believe was over when we heard shouting coming from Rosa's house.

"Margo, do you ever think about what you would take if you had to leave your home? What if the sheriff posted a sign on your front door and forced you to leave? What would you take?"

I looked at Rosa. Her eyes had tears in them, which told me she wanted more than a make-believe answer.

"I would take as many clothes as I could carry, some soap and my toothbrush, my postcard collection, and you."

Rosa gave me half a smile, sniffed to stop her nose from dripping, then sighed. Our eyes met and

I smiled. I wanted her to know that nothing could ever separate us. Well, I didn't think so until the shouting at Rosa's house grew into loud screams.

Rosa's eyes grew wide and watery again. "I'd better go," she said. She ran out of my room and down the steps. The screen door slammed behind her. I sat at the window facing her porch.

I was beginning to wonder if it was the darkness or something else out there that I was afraid of.

# Chapter 9

## DOMINOES

The arguing at Rosa's continued long after she'd gone home. I couldn't sleep. Charlie had gone to bed shortly after dinner and was snoring softly. The house was quiet except for Mama and Papa's talking. I sat on the top step and listened.

"I have enough flour to bake bread during the week," said Mama. "I will need flour next week."

"I will go into town for the flour," said Papa. His voice sounded unusually soft.

I knew that "going into town," instead of to Frappa's store, meant that Papa would stand in the long line of people who were also waiting for a fifty-pound sack of flour. I'd waited in line with him several times. The walk home was always a quiet one. I suspected the heavy weight of the sack on Papa's shoulder was not the only thing that bothered him.

"They continue to cut more work hours. How can a man support his family working one day a week?" Papa was talking about Mr. Meglio. "He is not angry with his family. He is a proud man who is willing to work—it is hard to accept handouts. His anger comes from a sad heart."

I understood what Papa was saying because Miss Dobson had explained "dominoes" to our class. She told us that a very large number of people worked in the steel mill. When the mill cut the workers' hours back, they had less money to spend. If they didn't have the money to spend, they couldn't afford to buy as much food or clothing, or to pay their bills. Then the businesses where they bought had fewer and fewer customers—like the banks, the grocery stores, and Papa's store.

I remember Miss Dobson saying, "When one domino fails to stay up, it causes a chain reaction, knocking the others down one by one." She told us that was how the problems of the Great Depression had grown worse. The big businesses would have to grow stronger before the smaller businesses could stay up.

I supposed Miss Dobson knew all this because she read her father's newspaper every day. I didn't think the dominoes had started to fall at Mr. Dobson's business. I always saw people in Johnstown's Central Park carrying a newspaper. I'd even seen men asleep on the park benches covered with the newspaper.

"It grows more difficult each week." Papa's voice caught my attention. "I cannot turn away people who bring me work. There are those who can pay, and there are those who want to pay. What can I do? Should I turn away the father who needs a buckle for his child's shoe, when the shoe is already two sizes too small? Do I turn away the farmer who offers me two bushels of apples for a pair of soles, when the bottom of each shoe has a hole the size of my fist?"

"The bills from the bank . . ." I couldn't hear all that Mama was saying.

"We have nothing to be ashamed of. We ask for help and we give help," said Papa in a firm voice.

I supposed that was why Mama insisted we open the back door to the men who knocked at it. They were usually the hoboes who got out of the boxcars when the train stopped at the brickyard. They used to jump down from the raised trestle. Now they used a wooden ladder someone had hammered into the wall next to the tracks—nobody in the neighborhood knew who put it there, and nobody wanted to take it down.

I remembered one day a boy just a little older than me came to our back door. He told Mama he'd gladly work for a bite to eat. It must have been hard for Mama, because she stood there for a long time and didn't say a word.

The boy finally said, "Sorry to have bothered you, ma'am. Your house has the mark on it. I'll go now."

Something he said or did woke Mama up from her daydream because she grabbed him by the arm and said, "No, no, *figlio mio*, my son. I'll make you a sandwich while you take that laundry off the clothesline for me. You can set it in that basket on the ground."

Papa insisted that Mama give the hoboes a small job when they asked. "It lets them swallow their food with dignity," he always said.

I remembered how Mama made the young man two large sandwiches, then sent me outside to give them to him. He had the clothes neatly folded and stacked in the basket. "Gee, thanks," I said, "that would have been my job. You can sit on the porch and eat."

He was very polite and explained that he wouldn't have troubled us, except that the mark on the brick foundation of our front porch was a sign the other hoboes put there to say it was okay to knock on our door. When he left, I looked for the mark in the spot where he mentioned. It was there in chalk—a circle with an *X* in the center. When I showed Papa later that evening, he went out and traced it in white paint. It's still there.

Mama and Papa were talking very softly now. I couldn't hear them. I crawled into bed and pulled the blanket over my shoulders. The November air was getting chilly. I was just about to close my eyes when I heard a door open. I looked out the window facing Rosa's front porch. Mr. Meglio was walking down his front steps, carrying a small bindle like the hoboes. I knew then and there what I'd been so afraid of. It wasn't the dark. It was the dominoes. The dominoes that had started to fall at the steel mill had reached Maple Avenue.

# Chapter 10

~·~

## THE ASSIGNMENT

I could feel the lack of sleep in everything I did on Sunday. Our house was filled with people all afternoon as they stopped by after church. Papa played his mandolin and the neighbors sang along, "Oh Marie, oh Marie . . ." I'm sure Mrs. Meglio could hear the singing, but she never came over with Rosa or Michael. Mama needed my help. I didn't see Rosa at all. The whole day passed in slow motion.

~·~

The next morning Rosa was waiting for me on her front steps, as she always did. The walk to school was usually a quiet one on Monday mornings. Today Rosa surprised me with her constant chatter. She talked about everything and everyone except her father. I was relieved to walk into our classroom. I wanted so much to ask Rosa if she would have to move, but she never gave me a chance to get one word in.

We took our seats in time to see Miss Dobson hand a stack of newspapers to Lola Nola. Lola has bright-red hair, and freckles. She stepped on a boy's toe—I heard it crunch—when he said, "Hurry up, Freckle Face." She got to my desk and smiled. "I guess he won't be playing dodgeball at recess," she said.

Miss Dobson used the newspapers and a map of the world to teach geography. She probably knew most of us would never leave Johnstown, Pennsylvania, but it was as though she cast a spell on us when she taught. Sometimes I would close my eyes in class while she talked about the customs and foods of different countries. I pictured it all in my mind. Someday, maybe someday, I would really be there.

Today all eyes were on Rosa in geography class. Especially every time she raised her hand and gave a little "Ooh-ooh," to answer one of Miss Dobson's questions. It worked twice. Then Miss Dobson told Rosa to collect the newspapers. Rosa kept smiling the whole time, as if nothing unusual had happened to her family. At recess she just continued smiling and talking, and never once mentioned her father. I was getting really annoyed. We usually talked to each other about everything.

Another set of newspapers was passed out at the end of history class, just before dismissal. Miss Dobson was writing an assignment in huge letters that spread across the board from one end to the other. Chalk dust flew through the air, casting a white film on her fingers and speckling her black shoes. A loud squeak of the chalk on the board brought the entire class to attention.

LETTERS DUE ON WEDNESDAY,
CORRECTED ON THURSDAY, MAILED ON FRIDAY.
STAMPS WILL BE PROVIDED.

"Class, I have saved these old newspapers for a reason. They are all from different days and months, and date back to March fifth, the day after President Roosevelt's inauguration. His dream is to pull our country out of this terrible state of poverty. He continues to work hard, as does our First Lady, Eleanor Roosevelt. They remain confident that this can be done. So must you and I. Therefore, your assignment is to study the newspaper in front of you. Take it home with you. Trade papers if you must. You are to find an article written about a person who inspires you, a person who has done something to support our country and President Roosevelt's belief that better times are ahead. Then you are to write a letter to that person. Let the person know how he or she has inspired you."

I had to admit, the newspaper sitting on my desk had me wondering. That day had the quietest dismissal I'd ever seen—especially after Miss Dobson told us the assignment would be our only history grade this term.

# Chapter 11

~

## BAD NEWS

"You wouldn't kid me, would you? This assignment is a cinch!" exclaimed Rosa.

She held the heavy wooden doors for me as we left Maple Avenue School. One whole day, and she still hadn't said a word about moving or about her father leaving. Now she was going on and on about the assignment.

"I don't even need the newspaper, I know exactly who I'm writing to," said Rosa. "Last year Amelia Earhart became the first woman to fly solo across the Atlantic Ocean. It took her thirteen hours and thirteen minutes. Can you imagine sitting in one spot all that time with nobody to talk to? I'd be so bored that I'd never be able to keep my eyes open. I think I'll tell her what an inspiration she is to me. She showed the world that women can set daring and dangerous records, too."

I purposely walked faster, which usually annoyed Rosa. Not today.

"I think I'll even tell her how I stay awake in Mr. Molar's English class by telling myself jokes. I just might include a few of those jokes to help Amelia stay awake the next time she sets a record." Rosa finally stopped talking.

I was just about to say "Rosa, what kind of record are you trying to set?" or "Rosa, I know about your father." I never got the chance.

As we neared home, we both saw Mama at the same time. She was walking out of Rosa's front door, carrying the pot she uses to deliver soup or pasta to neighbors who need help. A car was parked at the curb outside Rosa's house. A well-dressed woman was carrying a basket of clothes up the sidewalk to Rosa's front door.

"Here," was all Rosa said. She handed her newspaper to me and took all three of her front-porch stairs in one leap, practically knocking Mama and the woman off their feet.

Mama never said a word as we climbed our own porch stairs. I held the door open for her, and she kissed my forehead as she walked past me. That was when I noticed her tear-stained cheeks. Everything was all mixed up. Rosa had never stopped talking all day, and here was Mama as quiet as could be.

Something kept me from going to Rosa's to see if

she could play. Instead I stood at our door watching and waiting, hoping she would come to my house. I had been standing there for quite some time when Mama finally started to talk.

"Margo, come away from the door and set the table, please. Your papa will be home soon." Mama was stirring a small pot of soup with the long silver ladle she had brought from her mother's kitchen in Italy. It wasn't a fancy ladle, not like sterling silver. But Mama treasured it the way Papa had treasured his gold pocket watch. The only time the ladle ever left the stove was to get washed.

While Mama was calling Charlie to dinner, I lifted the lid and glanced into the pot. The water was bubbling very slowly. The chopped celery, tomato, onion, and carrots danced around the bare bone sitting on the bottom like a rock. No meat for the fourth day in a row. I breathed in deeply. It still smelled delicious. If I closed my eyes real tight, I could pretend I smelled the meat, too.

Papa, Charlie, and Mama all came through the front door together as I tucked the last napkin into its place. I was happy Papa was home. He always listened to the news, so he might think of someone for me to write to.

But dinner was exceptionally quiet. Mama kept looking at Papa, who said very little. Charlie kept looking at me as though he wanted to tell me something important. I decided it might be best to check the newspapers—the one Miss Dobson had given me, and the one Rosa had given me—before bothering Papa with my assignment.

I was in my room with the newspapers spread across the floor when Charlie came in.

"Margo, it's all my fault," he said as he sat on my bed.

"Don't worry, Charlie. Papa isn't really angry about the watch. Someone will know how to fix it."

"I'm not talking about the watch, Margo. I'm talking about the letter Papa received from the bank. It was signed by Mr. Lockhard. I wasn't going to tell you, especially because I got you in trouble over the watch, but . . ."

My heart was racing, and I could feel the blood rushing to my face. "What letter, Charlie?"

"It was delivered on Saturday while I was helping Papa. I couldn't understand why he was pulling papers out of the file in his desk and checking his bank book. I peeked while he was helping a customer. The letter said we're six months behind in payments, and Papa is to make an appointment with Mr. Lockhard immediately."

"How could this possibly be your fault, Charlie?"

"My leg. I saw the papers. Papa borrowed five thousand dollars for the doctor to come from Boston. He had to agree to sign over the house, the store, and everything we own as collateral for the loan. I saw it; Papa signed his name at the bottom."

I sat next to Charlie and put my arm around his shoulder. I knew Mama and Papa had never meant for Charlie or me to see those papers, or they would have been in the drawer with Papa's medal, the citizenship papers, and the scattered watch pieces.

"That's why Papa was so quiet at dinner. He went to see Mr. Lockhard this afternoon," added Charlie. His chin puckered up and his lower lip quivered.

The soup I ate at dinner bubbled inside my stomach, and I swallowed hard to keep it from coming back up. I finally understood why Mama had been crying. I cleared my throat and spoke very slowly so that my voice wouldn't shake. I wouldn't let Charlie know how frightened I was.

"Charlie, this is not your fault. The accident was not your fault. The Great Depression is not your fault. It's dominoes—when one thing goes wrong, other things fall right behind it no matter how hard or how fast you work to stop them."

A cold chill ran down my spine. I pulled Charlie

closer to me and wrapped a blanket around the two of us.

What I didn't tell my little brother was that the fallen dominoes had worked their way right up Maple Avenue, to our front porch.

# Chapter 12

## VICTORY MEDAL

As usual, Charlie was snoring away, only this time he had cried himself to sleep on my bed. I sat on the floor and continued to scan the newspapers. I knew Mama and Papa would talk once they thought Charlie and I were asleep.

It was hard to think about my assignment, so I quietly turned the pages of the newspaper and looked at the pictures. One photo in particular caught my attention. It was a picture of some women seated around Mrs. Roosevelt. The article underneath was written by E. D. Kirby. It mentioned that Mrs. Roosevelt had held a press conference for women journalists just two days after her husband's inauguration.

The sound of chairs scraping against the floor interrupted my reading. Mama and Papa were sitting down at the dining room table. I walked softly to the top step and sat.

"I think Charlie may have seen the letter." Papa's voice was just above a whisper. "It was foolish of me to think we could hide it forever. We came so close to losing him. I would do it all again if I had to. The doctor from Boston was the best answer."

"It was the only thing to do," answered Mama. "Margo and Charlie had to find out sooner or later. They are older now and will understand."

The dishes in the china cabinet rattled as Papa slammed his hand down on the table. "How can I ask my children to understand if I can't understand?" Papa's voice grew louder. "It isn't the money for the operation, it's the sorrow I see in the eyes of those I pass on the street. It's the hungry children I see standing in line for the soup kitchen. It's the anger and frustration I hear coming from a neighbor's home. And it's the heartache I feel when I can't even afford a pound of peanut butter kisses for my children."

I heard Papa's chair scrape the floor and the drawer of the server open. I slid down three steps to where I could peek out from behind the railing. The deep crease in Papa's brow and the misty look in his eyes made me swallow back the lump in my throat. Papa pulled out the medal and papers he cherished and clenched them tightly in his hands.

"This medal was given to me when I fought in the Great War and earned my citizenship of this country," he said. "I was Margo's age in Italy when I dreamed of coming to the United States. I close my eyes and still see the tears people cried as our ship passed the Statue of Liberty. There must be an answer for us now. Nobody will take our home." Papa lifted the Victory Medal he had been awarded by the army and dangled it in the air by its ribbon. He stared at it. Then he tightened his fingers around the circular bronze medal until his hand shook.

I could no longer fight back the tears. A sob escaped my lips. Papa turned and saw me. He and Mama were out of their seats and up the stairs in no time. They sat next to me on the steps, cradling me in their arms. Mama looked up and noticed Charlie standing at the top of the stairs. He must have heard everything, because Mama was wiping tears from his eyes when he sat next to me.

"Margo and Charlie, there is more we must tell you," said Mama.

Papa began, "Charlie, you saw the papers?"

"Yes, Papa."

"Then you know everything except one thing. If your Mama and I had to make a decision for Margo's health, we would find the best doctor with the best solution. We would do what we did for you. There was no right or wrong, there was only one answer—to find the doctor who could save your life, and your leg if possible. We would make the same decision all over again, Charlie. Now the bank wants the money I borrowed. We can't pay it because people don't always pay me in cash. We are never hungry because many of them pay with food from their farms. We will have canned goods all winter because they pay me with the fruit of their hard work. Again, there is no right or wrong. It is the only answer. The bank doesn't see it my way. I tried to explain, but they insist on money I don't have and payments I can't meet. They will give us two weeks to catch up on back payments."

"You must tell them the rest," said Mama as she reached across Charlie and me and took Papa's hand in hers.

Papa sighed. "Tomorrow a sign will be posted on our front door, a sheriff sale sign. You know what that means. You must remember this is your home, and we have two weeks. You hold your head high when you go in and out that door."

I was determined not to cry. Just two days ago Rosa had asked me what I would take with me if I had to leave. Well, now I knew two things for sure. I would never leave, and there had to be a way to help Papa save our home. I might be just a kid, but I would find somebody to listen to me.

Papa looked at Charlie and me. I could see he was just as determined. "Margo, there was a small ray of hope when Charlie needed help, and we found it. Charlie, the doctors thought it would take a miracle for you to get well, and it happened. We can do it again. Margo, you hold this for me while Mama and I find the answer. It will give us all courage." Papa opened his fingers and gently placed the medal in my hand.

# Chapter 13

## TUESDAY

"My letter is done, Margo."

Rosa leaned over my school desk and looked at me as if she expected me to announce the same. The truth was that I hadn't even thought about the assignment after Papa had given me the medal. I slept with it under my pillow. Now it was tucked in the pocket of my dress. I intended to keep it with me all the time.

"I sent Amelia Earhart a thank-you letter, Margo. I told her she has been an inspiration to all young women, especially those who like to travel. I explained our game of make-believe and told her that now we can pretend we're in the plane with her. I also told her that she should try to be the first woman to fly around the world. Margo, I asked her to send me a postcard when she does fly around the world. I'll give it to you."

"Thank you, Rosa." I was relieved to hear she hadn't sent any of her silly jokes. I didn't have the heart to tell her she might have to find another friend with a postcard collection.

The day grew worse. Everybody was writing to somebody. One person wrote to Babe Ruth and congratulated him for winning the World Series last year. He asked Babe Ruth to help find his papa and point him in the right direction—home. Miss Dobson almost made him remove that sentence.

But then she said, "Determination will turn this country around. Babe Ruth took two strikes before he pointed and told a crowd where the next pitch would land. Who knows, maybe he could point lost folks back toward home."

I snuck a quick peek at Rosa when Miss Dobson said that. Her smile was still there, as wide as the Mississippi!

Lola Nola wrote to President Roosevelt and told him that his Fireside Chats were the best. She especially liked the one about the outdoor work camp for boys ages eighteen to twenty-five. She told the President that she was the only girl in a family of eight children, and that he could have three of her older brothers. She promised the President they would work hard, and her mother wouldn't mind at all if most of their pay was sent home to help out with the younger children. She did ask the President if he minded that she'd call the camp the CCC since she couldn't spell Civilian Conservation Corps without help from Miss Dobson.

Many letters were already written and turned in. I didn't have a clue whom I'd write to.

At dismissal, I told Rosa I had to run right home because Mama needed my help. Charlie must have had the same idea. He was halfway home when I caught up with him.

We could see the SHERIFF SALE sign before we crossed the street. So could everybody else. Mrs. DiLuso was standing outside Frappa's Grocery Store, talking to another person and looking over at our house.

Maybe it was the way she was shaking her head that made me do what I did. Charlie was two steps ahead of me. I yanked on his jacket and pulled him back beside me. I stuck my hand in my pocket and felt for the medal. It was there. Good.

"Come on, Charlie. We're going in to visit with Mr. Frappa." I kept a grip on Charlie's jacket, held my head high, and steered my little brother toward Frappa's store.

I ignored Mrs. DiLuso when she made that funny clicking noise with her tongue and said, "Poor children. I told their mama Maple Avenue would have its problems."

Mr. Frappa must have seen us coming, because he was holding two peanut butter kisses and he gave us each one. He never said a word about the sign. He just talked to us about anything and everything. I considered asking him if he knew how I could help Mama and Papa. But then I realized the two peanut butter kisses *were* his way of helping. Instead I told him about my assignment.

"Margo, if you have any interest in writing or traveling someday, read the newspaper articles written by E. D. Kirby. Kirby is a local journalist who travels to New York on occasion. I'll bet you find someone interesting to write to if you read those articles."

"E. D. Kirby. That was the name on an article I started reading last night. I guess I'll read it again."

Charlie was licking his fingers, sticky from the peanut butter kiss. "You know, Mr. Frappa, you must have been one great teacher. I wish you were a teacher here at Maple Avenue."

Mr. Frappa burst out laughing. "I thought I was, Charlie. I thought I was."

Charlie and I headed home just in time to see Rosa walking up her front stairs. She stood dead still when she glanced over and saw the sign on our door.

Finally she looked at me and said, "See you tomorrow, Margo."

## Chapter 14

## THE LETTER

The late afternoon and evening passed as though nothing had happened. Papa brought home two jars of canned tomatoes—payment for a stitched boot. Mama made dinner and we all talked about our day. I watched Mama and Papa, looking for signs of that small ray of hope they believed in. I made certain the medal was in my pocket just in case Papa asked for it. He didn't.

I hadn't mentioned my assignment to Papa. He had enough to worry about. The newspapers were still opened on the floor of my bedroom. Lola Nola had also given me her newspaper after Miss Dobson had approved her letter. I scanned the pages.

All three issues had an article by E. D. Kirby. One was about the apple peddlers in New York City. It mentioned how many of the men selling apples on the street corners had been engineers, mechanics, bankers, and stockbrokers. It showed a picture of a man dressed in a suit selling apples for a nickel.

The second article was about teachers. Schools across the United States continued to close because the teachers could not be paid. Kirby wrote that children my age were starving—for food and for education.

The picture I had seen last night caught my attention. The article was titled "First Lady Holds a First." It described how Eleanor Roosevelt had held a press conference for women journalists, and how she had been writing for newspapers and magazines since the 1920s. It went on to explain how other presidents' wives had avoided the press, while Eleanor believed that the American people should know what was happening in the White House. Mrs. Roosevelt would be helping the President. She wanted to see for herself how the American people were getting along. She would focus particular attention on the American youth. The final sentence E. D. Kirby wrote was, "Mrs. Roosevelt has received hundreds of letters requesting help. She intends to have each one answered."

I grabbed the page of the newspaper and read it again. There it was in black and white, the answer to my assignment. That wasn't all. I had found someone who was willing to listen to an American girl . . . to an eleven-year-old . . . someone who would listen to me. I must have looked pretty silly kissing the picture of Eleanor Roosevelt over and over again.

I glanced at the picture of the President's wife one more time. My smile faded away when the words popped out at me: "Mrs. Roosevelt has received hundreds of letters requesting help."

I sat on the trunk under my window and looked out over Maple Avenue. My letter would be one of hundreds to Mrs. Roosevelt, maybe even one in a million by the time it got to her. But in Papa's words, it was the only answer.

I knew a small ray of hope when I saw one.

# Chapter 15

## WEDNESDAY

I placed my letter to Mrs. Roosevelt on Miss Dobson's desk after history class.

"Do you feel well, Margo?" Miss Dobson searched my eyes as though she could see straight through to what was on my mind.

My assignment was the last to be handed in. I had spent most of the night writing and rewriting.

"I'll be okay, Miss Dobson. I'm sorry I fell asleep in math class." I knew my ears were burning red. I'd never heard Miss Dobson dismiss the class for recess. She'd let me sleep right there at my desk, with my math book as a pillow for my head. I'd woken up to Rosa nudging me in the arm. "Rise and shine. Wake up, sleepyhead. You missed a good game of dodgeball and some excitement at recess."

I'd made certain I'd sat straight in my seat for the

rest of the day. Now here I was face-to-face with Miss Dobson.

"I'll be happy to stay after school and make up the work I missed in math class." I was in no rush to go home. The SHERIFF SALE sign would still be there.

"I'm trying to understand something, Margo," said Miss Dobson. "Usually you are the lively, smiling face in this class, and Rosa is the quiet one at your side. Something has turned that all around. I'm amazed Rosa's cheekbones aren't hurting from all her smiling. As for Charlie, well, he got into a fight on the playground at recess."

"Oh, Charlie!" I bit my lip to keep from saying out loud all the things that raced through my mind. "I suppose we'll both be staying after school today."

"No," said Miss Dobson. "When the principal came looking for you, he found you asleep at your desk. He agreed that something unusual was going on. He said you could meet Charlie in his office at dismissal. You need not stay either, Margo. You can complete the math problems on page two hundred thirty to catch up with the rest of the class. Try to get a good rest tonight."

I thanked Miss Dobson, gathered my books, and was leaving, when she called me back to her desk.

"Margo." She put her arm around my shoulder.

"These are difficult times. Perhaps I can help if you tell me . . ."

I never heard the end of her sentence. Our eyes locked and for a moment I hoped that maybe she really could see straight through to what was on my mind. I knew she cared, and I knew she would do her best to help . . . but her best could never be enough. Not this time. Teachers everywhere were going through desperate times, too. After all, her father's newspaper said so.

"Thanks anyway, Miss Dobson." I turned and walked out the door. I couldn't wait to get my hands on Charlie.

I walked down to the principal's office. The school secretary saw me and said, "You may go, Charlie." The principal was in his office yelling. I could see the backs of two heads through the opaque glass.

Charlie took one look at my face and said, "I didn't start it. They were making fun of the sheriff sale sign on our door."

"Who was making fun?" I wasn't about to let Charlie off the hook.

"Double and Trouble. That's them in the principal's office." Charlie stuck his thumb to his nose and wiggled his fingers at them. I grabbed him by the arm and yanked him out the office door, grateful that Lola's brothers couldn't see him.

"They started it," Charlie insisted as we walked

down the hall. "They said it was a good thing we have friends at St. Anthony's Orphanage, 'cause that's where we'll be living after Mama and Papa get arrested for all the money they owe."

"That isn't true, Charlie, and I don't care what they said. The last thing Mama and Papa need is to know you got in a fight. You get to tell Mama and Papa this one, and don't expect me to stick up for you." We stepped out into the cool air. I aimed a good hard kick at a stone sitting outside the door. It landed with a loud clunk against the black wrought-iron fence surrounding the playground.

"Where were you, anyway? I could have used your help at recess, you know." Charlie had a way of turning things around.

"Oh no you don't, Charlie." I stopped in the middle of the sidewalk and pointed my finger right at Charlie's nose. "This is your own fault. Nobody told you to start a war over a stupid sign."

"Well, we don't really need to tell Mama and Papa," said Charlie. He gave me one of his big-brown-eyes looks. "The principal said it was about time someone popped one of the Nola brothers a good shot in the stomach. But he made me promise not to get into any more fights on the playground. He said he wouldn't tell Mama and Papa because you'd probably take care of things once you found out."

"Well, we'll just see about that." And that was all

I could say. I considered telling Charlie he should have aimed for the nose instead of the stomach.

The more I thought about everything, the faster I walked. Charlie was behind me, and as far as I was concerned, he could stay there.

Enough was enough! I ignored Rosa when she called to me from her front porch. I ignored Mama and Papa when they looked up from the dining room table to say hello. I ignored the fact that Papa was home early and that the table was covered with account books and papers. I didn't even flinch when I noticed that Mama's eyes were red again.

I paid no heed to Papa's "Margo!" as I stomped up the stairs to my room and slammed my door shut as hard as I could. I didn't pay any attention to my growling stomach when Mama called me to dinner. I simply told her I wasn't hungry and stayed in my room.

It was bedtime when Charlie knocked on my door and whispered, "Margo, I'm really sorry. Can I come in?" I didn't answer him; instead I threw my pillow as hard as I could. It landed with a loud thud against the door, then fell to the floor.

I thought I'd feel better. I didn't. I was hungry. I was tired—tired of being mad at everyone. But there was something far worse than the anger pounding away inside my head. It was the feeling in my heart. I was lonely, very lonely.

Now I understood Rosa's happy face. It hurt too much to be angry.

I opened my window and looked beyond the rooftops across the street. My friends the stars were waiting for me. I wondered, *Are there as many letters written to Mrs. Roosevelt as there are stars in the sky? Millions of stars . . . millions of people who need help . . .*

I remembered Papa's medal in my pocket. I pulled it out. *Courage. Courageous.* I could say it and I could spell it. But could I ever *be* it? I had to find a way to get my letter delivered to Mrs. Roosevelt in time, even if I had to ride the boxcars myself.

I held Papa's medal up to the night sky. It sparkled brighter than the stars above the rooftops. Could I ever dare to . . . Had the answer been in my pocket all this time?

I closed my window and crawled into bed. There were too many questions and not enough answers. But I knew one thing for sure. Tomorrow would be a better day.

# Chapter 16

## THE DELIVERY

Rosa sat on her porch steps waiting for me. She smiled. I smiled back. We started walking. Charlie and Michael were a block ahead of us.

"Margo, you never told me what you wrote in your letter. Who did you write to?" Rosa the Curious was back.

I wanted to say "You never gave me a chance to tell you" or "Why didn't you wait for me after school yesterday?" Instead I smiled and answered, "I wrote to the First Lady, Eleanor Roosevelt."

Rosa looked pretty funny standing in the middle of the sidewalk with her mouth wide open and her eyes bulging.

"Stop your gawking," I said with a chuckle. "Come on, we'll be late for school." I tried to pull her along.

Rosa wouldn't budge. "You wouldn't kid me, would you? Eleanor Everywhere? You wrote to Eleanor Everywhere?"

"Come on, Rosa. We'll be late." I walked ahead of her and realized she wasn't about to move. I turned back and said, "Okay, okay. If you promise to walk faster I'll tell you what I wrote in my letter."

I knew it would work.

I reminded Rosa that Mrs. Roosevelt had been writing for magazines and newspapers since the 1920s. "Well, now Eleanor Roosevelt writes about her travels and life in the White House. I thought she might be an inspiration to others. Well, at least she is to me. She travels, which I hope to do someday. She writes, which I like to do. And she's helping others, which we all need."

I didn't tell Rosa everything I had written in my letter. I wasn't sure if it was because we got to the classroom just in time again. Maybe I didn't tell her because I thought the First Lady couldn't help . . . or maybe I didn't want Rosa to tell me that Eleanor Roosevelt would be everywhere *other* than reading a letter from a young girl in Johnstown, Pennsylvania.

Miss Dobson returned our letters later that day. She gave us time to write our final drafts with all the necessary corrections. When everybody was done, she passed out envelopes and stamps. I couldn't understand how she had been able to find the addresses of famous people like Babe Ruth and Amelia Earhart. We folded our letters and placed them in the envelopes. Miss Dobson collected them for "one last check." It would be our responsibility to mail our letters at the post office the next day, after she had returned them to us. Rosa and I decided to mail our letters together.

"Let's have a contest, Margo. The one who gets a reply to her letter first has to carry the other person's books to and from school for a week." Rosa was always making up contests, especially if she thought she could win.

"It's a deal," I said. "I wonder if any of us will get a reply. Some of the letters are going to famous people a long way from Johnstown. It sure will be exciting to watch the bulletin board and map."

Miss Dobson had explained that as the replies came in, the student who wrote to that person could tack the letter on the bulletin board for everyone to read, and place a little flag on the city the reply came from. "A fine lesson in geography" was how she described it.

I was leaving school with Rosa when Miss Dobson called me back into the classroom. She told Rosa to go along home because she would need me for a while.

Miss Dobson sat at her desk and pulled my letter

from the pile. "Margo, your letter is well written. I hope you will think about journalism someday."

"Thank you, Miss Dobson."

"There is another reason why I wanted to speak with you, Margo. I know from your letter that you're hoping Mrs. Roosevelt can help your folks." Miss Dobson didn't look angry, but I could tell by the sound of her voice that something had bothered her.

My ears were burning. "I'm sorry, Miss Dobson, maybe I shouldn't have asked for help. I read an article in the newspaper by E. D. Kirby. It said that hundreds of people were writing to Mrs. Roosevelt and asking her for help. I just thought that maybe . . ."

"How much time has the bank given your father?"

"Mr. Lockhard told Papa he could have two weeks from the time he received the letter. It was delivered last Saturday. Papa has nine days left. Do you think Mrs. Roosevelt will get my letter in time?"

No answer. Miss Dobson tapped her pen on a date in her calendar book. There was something written there that I couldn't read. The tiny letters were blotched with ink.

"Miss Dobson?" Still no answer.

"There is a sheriff sale sign on my front door." The words came out in a whisper. Again no answer.

I could only think that maybe my letter should never have been written. My heartbeat matched the tapping of Miss Dobson's pen.

She looked at me for a second, then up at the ceiling. Her forehead was wrinkled, and her eyes were moving back and forth as if she were reading an answer written in the air above her. Then she let out a deep sigh.

"That's it!" was all she said before she looked back at me and said, "Margo, would you trust me to make certain your letter gets delivered?"

My mind must have temporarily lost track of where I was and whom I was talking to. It was the first time I'd ever hugged a teacher. I knew then that I could trust Miss Dobson to help me.

I gathered my books and thanked Miss Dobson. I walked halfway down the hall and stopped. My letter to Mrs. Roosevelt wasn't done. I'd known it last night, and it had been half on my mind all day.

I turned and walked back to the classroom. I knocked. "Miss Dobson?" She was clearing the top of her desk, moving books and papers around. She didn't hear me. I spoke more loudly. "Miss Dobson?"

She looked up and smiled. "Yes, Margo." My letter was in her hand.

"Miss Dobson, my letter isn't finished. Could I please add one more thing before you mail it?"

"You did a fine job with your letter, Margo. But

certainly if you feel the need to add something more, then you may." She opened my letter and watched as I wrote at the bottom under "Sincerely, Margo Bandini,"

*P.S. Mrs. Roosevelt, my papa earned this medal in the Great War. He gave it to me to hold until we can find an answer. He told me it gives him courage. If you can help us, please send it back to me so I can return it to Papa. If you cannot help us, I think you and President Roosevelt might need it more than my papa.*

> *Your friend,*
> *Margo*

I carefully placed Papa's Victory Medal in the envelope with my letter. Miss Dobson taped the envelope shut.

"Margo, I think you'll be an inspiration to each other."

"Thank you, Miss Dobson. But won't my letter need a few more stamps?"

I can still picture Miss Dobson's smile. She never answered me.

## Chapter 17

~~~

## RUNNING OUT OF TIME

It felt odd to me. After school last Friday, Papa sent me to Mr. Frappa's with the account book. He said the small change in his pocket wouldn't make a difference in Mr. Lockhard's register. Papa said, "Margo, it's better to give it to someone who understands how delicious one little peanut butter kiss can taste." Then he winked at me.

Charlie went to work with Papa on Saturday. Mrs. Meglio sat on her front porch most of the day, all bundled up in a sweater and blanket, folding clothes and stitching socks. Mama said Mrs. Meglio just sat and waited, hoping Mr. Meglio would hop off the train near the brickyard. Rosa had never mentioned her father. Nobody knew where he went. I couldn't be angry with her for not talking about him. I hadn't told her the complete truth when she asked where my letter was. I simply told her it was a long letter and weighed too much, so Miss Dobson had offered to mail it.

After dinner Rosa and I pretended we were in the plane with Amelia Earhart, sending postcards from all over the world. We were surprised to see the lady with the gray hat on the Saturday-night excursion train. It had been only one week since the last time we'd seen her.

Sunday was church as usual, company as usual, and mandolin music as usual. Mama surprised us with a homemade white cake. She said it was a reminder of the good times that had been, and a gesture of hope for better times to come. Mama had actually won a ribbon for her white cake recipe at St. Anthony's festival, before the dominoes had started to fall. She said that was how she wanted the neighbors on Maple Avenue to remember her.

The neighbors were trying to help. They stopped by to visit Mama more often but could offer nothing more than kind words. Mr. Frappa told me that many of them were worried a SHERIFF SALE sign would be posted on their doors next. The nuns from the orphanage told Charlie they were praying for a miracle to happen.

There was one good thing that happened. Mrs. DiLuso visited less often. Mama thought she was insulted because Mama told Mrs. DiLuso that *il diavolo* didn't arrive on the tail of a shooting star, but in the hearts of those who allowed it.

Monday night arrived, and everything still seemed normal. In five days the sheriff would stand at our front door and escort us out of the house.

It was hard for me to concentrate in school. Miss Dobson must have understood, because she never called on me. Papa was closing the store early this week. After school I met him and we waited in line for a sack of flour. On the way home, we saw Mrs. Meglio, Michael, and Rosa standing in line at the soup kitchen. Rosa put her head down when she saw me coming. I had to pass right by her, so I said, "See you tomorrow, Rosa."

Mama and Papa continued to search through the important papers that covered the table. Papa was at the bank early Tuesday morning. He said Mr. Lockhard still insisted that if we couldn't make the payments, the bank must collect our home. Papa cleared his throat loudly, then stood straight as a rod and imitated Mr. Lockhard. "It was an agreement, Mr. Bandini. You had ample time to locate funds for overdue payments. Two weeks was a courtesy to you and your family for good business relations . . . in the past, that is."

I knew Mama and Papa hadn't given up. When I arrived home from school, Papa was across the street using Mr. Frappa's telephone to try to contact a relative in Buffalo, New York. He never reached him.

At dinner Charlie asked if we would have to leave the table and chairs behind. Mama said she didn't think there was a suitcase big enough for them to fit in. I would never forget what happened next.

Papa started it all. He laughed and told Charlie not to worry. If the sheriff arrived, the only thing we had to take with us was Mama and her silver ladle. He said, "If I were the sheriff, I'd think twice about crossing your mama's path when that ladle is in her hand. She's an expert at stirring things up into a fine mix."

Then Charlie added, "If I were the sheriff, I'd think twice about crossing Mama's path when she's using a rolling pin to make the pasta dough. He might go away with an aching noodle!"

Then I added, "If I were the sheriff, I'd think twice about crossing Mama's path when she has a spatula in her hand. She might flatten him like a pancake."

It went on and on until our sides hurt from laughing so hard. Nobody would ever have guessed we were a family about to lose everything we owned.

"Good night, Mama. Good night, Papa. Charlie and I are going to bed," I called from the top step.

Mama blew a kiss.

"Margo," called Papa. "Remember, laughter will

soothe the aching heart, but courage will heal it. You still have the medal?"

I swallowed hard to steady my voice.

"The medal is tucked away in the best place I could think of, Papa."

# Chapter 18

## A Visitor

Rosa and I ran home from school every day, hoping for a reply. Rosa was certain Amelia Earhart would answer her letter first, because Mrs. Roosevelt was too busy traveling. I hadn't told Rosa that a letter after Saturday wouldn't make any difference anyway.

On Wednesday, several replies were posted on the bulletin board. They were mostly from local people who had received a letter from someone in the class. Little flags stood out on the map, all of them near the dot that showed Johnstown.

Just before recess I told Rosa to go ahead, that I'd be right out. I walked back to the map and put a finger on Johnstown. With the tip of my little finger I measured the distance to Pittsburgh. Papa said we would go to his cousin's house near Pittsburgh if we had to leave. We had visited there a long time ago, before Charlie's accident. All I could remember was that Papa's cousin had a big brown mole on her cheek, and she fed me a thin waffle cookie called a *pizelle*. Charlie said he'd rather live at the orphanage. Mama simply said we would all stay together, no matter what happened or where we went. Pittsburgh was six fingertips away.

Then I used my fingertip to measure how far it was from Johnstown to Washington, D.C. Sixteen fingertips! It was more than double the distance to Pittsburgh. In Pittsburgh I would be forever away from Rosa. But suddenly Mrs. Roosevelt felt an impossible distance away from me. Three days left. I looked at the map and wondered where my letter was in those sixteen fingertips.

~⟪~

I was still wondering late that night when I opened my window to count the stars. I didn't want to go to sleep. I was afraid there wouldn't be a window for me to look out of in Pittsburgh.

It wasn't any easier in the morning. Waking up meant one more day had gone by without a reply. My family was one day closer to leaving.

I couldn't eat breakfast. It was Thursday, one week since Miss Dobson had talked to me about my letter. No answer. Maybe Eleanor Everywhere was somewhere other than the White House.

The bulletin board was the main attraction every

morning when we got to school. There was another reply. It was the first one to arrive from outside Pennsylvania. I was surprised to see that it was from E. D. Kirby and had been sent from New York City.

When the others walked away, I started to count how many fingertips to New York City. I wondered if it was as far as Washington, D.C.

"What are you doing?" I didn't hear Rosa come up behind me. I turned and tried to think of a quick answer. "Margo, your face is all red." Rosa was staring at me as if I had the chicken pox.

"Oh, I'm just happy to know somebody in our class wrote to the same journalist I hope to be like someday." Rosa knew I looked for articles written by E. D. Kirby every time I went into Mr. Frappa's. He let me scan the newspaper without buying it. But it wasn't enough of an answer for Rosa the Curious.

"So why should that make you turn beet-red?" she pressed further.

"Well, the truth is, I was thinking that if a letter got to New York City and a reply has returned that quickly, then maybe one of us will hear real soon, too." I looked Rosa right in the eyes and never flinched.

"Ah-ha!" she shouted. "So you think you can still win. Well, I hope you're prepared to carry my books, because *I'm* going to win. Amelia Earhart is probably checking the weather right now. I think she just might fly right over Maple Avenue and drop-deliver her reply to me personally."

It sure did feel good to laugh.

At dismissal Rosa challenged me to a race from the playground to my front porch. At first I said no because I wanted to stay and tell Miss Dobson that tomorrow would be my last day of school. I decided it could wait.

"On your mark," yelled Charlie and Michael together, "get set . . . go!"

Rosa and I ran practically side by side all the way down Maple Avenue.

"I'll bet there's a reply sitting right on my front porch." Rosa was out of breath.

"Yeah?" I shouted. "Maybe you'd better check the roof of your front porch first, if you think it was drop-delivered. But don't rush or anything, because I'll still get to mine first. I'm going to win this race."

We were laughing so hard that neither one of us noticed the sheriff's car parked outside my house. It wasn't until Rosa yanked at my dress to keep me from reaching my porch that I looked up. We stopped laughing.

"I'll always be your friend, Margo." Rosa looked at me through big tears and ran back to her house.

My feet wouldn't move. I could hear Papa's voice inside.

I turned to hear Charlie ask, "Who won, Margo?"

I couldn't answer. I couldn't move. I couldn't protect my little brother from the bad news.

Charlie noticed the car. "Come on, Margo. Mama and Papa will need our help."

# Chapter 19

~~~~~

## THE REPLY

Mama was seated at the table next to the sheriff, who was in a gray uniform. I had seen him just one other time. It was the day he'd shown up to force the family down the street out of their home. His eyes darted back and forth from Mr. Lockhard to Papa.

Papa was sitting at the head of the table, where he always sat. Mr. Lockhard was dressed in a striped suit and was seated across from Mama. Charlie walked right over to Mama and stood by her side. He put his arm around Mama's shoulder.

I stayed at the door, wondering if Mr. Lockhard could hear my heart pounding. I bit my lower lip to keep from screaming at them. I wanted the sheriff and Mr. Lockhard to go away. We still had two more days before we'd have to leave.

"Come, Margo. We have visitors." Papa motioned for me to sit next to Mr. Lockhard.

I ignored the empty seat and walked over to Papa. Papa pulled me onto his lap and put an arm around me, just as he did when I was five. I felt safe.

Mr. Lockhard cleared his throat, straightened his suit jacket, then began, "It appears, Miss Bandini, that you have been busy writing a letter to Mrs. Roosevelt." He looked at me as if I might try to squirm my way out of trouble.

I didn't like Mr. Lockhard, and from the look on his face, I knew he didn't like me. But I wasn't about to squirm, not even when Papa said, "You did what, Margo?"

"I wrote a letter to Eleanor Roosevelt." I blurted it out, then looked at everybody seated at the table. They just stared at me as if I should explain more.

"I had to write to somebody for an assignment, so I wrote to Mrs. Roosevelt," I said again. "I told her everything that's happened to us."

I thought there would be a million questions, like "Why?" or "What did you think she could do?" or even "How did you get a letter to Mrs. Roosevelt?" Instead there was dead silence in the room.

Seconds raced by, and still nobody said a word. Then I knew why. I remembered the hobo, when Charlie had been missing—the last time I'd thought I could help. I'd almost had all of Maple Avenue chasing the Gypsies out of town. My lips started to quiver. "Oh no," I whispered.

Mama was sitting with her head down. Was she praying? Charlie had a confused look on his face, and Papa just sat there with one arm around me.

I looked right into Papa's eyes and said, "I was just trying to help. I didn't know what else to do. I was just trying to help, Papa." A tear slipped down my cheek. "This is our home." Another tear fell on Papa's arm. "Nobody should be allowed to force us to leave, not when you and Mama have helped so many other people."

Mr. Lockhard cleared his throat more loudly this time and added, "Well, Miss Bandini, hmmm, well, it appears that Mrs. Roosevelt agrees with you. She received your letter on Sunday."

I looked at Mr. Lockhard, and then over at the sheriff, who actually smiled at me.

Mama's eyes filled with tears, but it was the same look she had when Charlie walked through the door the day he came home from the hospital.

Charlie still looked confused.

Mr. Lockhard continued. "Just today her staff contacted me at the bank concerning your family's loan. In fact, I had the pleasure of a brief conversation with the First Lady herself." He cleared his throat again, then dabbed his forehead with a handkerchief. "I must admit, it was a conversation I'll always remember, thanks to you and your letter."

Papa looked at me and winked. Then, without a word, he gave me another look to let me know that we would discuss later what I'd written in my letter.

Mr. Lockhard pulled on the chain of his pocket watch, then opened it to check the time. He sat poker straight at the edge of his chair as though he was remembering that time and a bank president must never slow down. He continued more rapidly, "I assured Mrs. Roosevelt that I would personally deliver her reply to you and your family. I'd also like to thank the sheriff for driving your father and me here to your fine home. My bank has worked out a plan that will help your father with the loan. The sign will be removed from your front door, and you can rest assured that your family still has a home and a business to care for."

My head and shoulders collapsed against Papa's chest. I didn't realize I had stopped breathing while Mr. Lockhard was talking. Mama and Charlie ran to Papa and me. I was still gasping while Mama, Papa, and Charlie smothered me with hugs. The four of us were laughing and crying at the good news.

"This will always be our home?" I asked as soon as I could speak.

"For as long as you choose to live here. Yes, this will be your home." I think I caught a smile under Mr. Lockhard's mustache.

Mr. Lockhard stood up. "That must have been quite a letter. I'm proud to know you, Miss Bandini. What you did took a great deal of courage." He shook my hand and added, "Oh yes, Mrs. Roosevelt asked that I remind you to contact E. D. Kirby for the remainder of her message."

The sheriff and Mr. Lockhard walked behind Papa as he led them out the door. Papa ripped the SHERIFF SALE sign off the door and gave it back to the sheriff. Mr. Lockhard didn't say a word; he just shook my papa's hand.

# Chapter 20

## E. D. KIRBY

Friday was always exciting, but that Friday was like a brand-new beginning. Miss Dobson had me stand up in front of the class and explain my whole story. They clapped when I told them we'd be staying on Maple Avenue.

There was one small detail that a boy in my class reminded me of—How would I get Papa's Victory Medal back? I sure hoped E. D. Kirby could help me with that answer.

At dismissal I told Rosa I'd have to hurry to Mr. Frappa's to see if he knew how I could contact E. D. Kirby.

"I have to get Papa's medal back to him. He doesn't even know I don't have it," I told Rosa.

Just as I was bolting out the door, Miss Dobson called me back and asked me to sit. I had to wait until the other students were gone.

"Thank you again, Miss Dobson. I don't know how you got my letter delivered to Mrs. Roosevelt so quickly. I'm just in a little hurry because Mr. Frappa might be able to tell me how to reach E. D. Kirby. I hope Mr. Kirby can tell me how to get Papa's medal back."

"Margo, what makes you think E. D. Kirby is a man?"

"Well, I don't know, I . . ."

Miss Dobson was smiling. "Please come here, Margo."

I walked over to Miss Dobson's desk. She was pulling an envelope and a picture from her desk drawer. She set the picture in front of me.

"That's the same picture from my newspaper article, except it's bigger." I was surprised to see writing in the bottom corner. I read it out loud.

TO MY FRIEND AND WRITING COMPANION,
ELAINE DOBSON KIRBY
WITH LOVE, ELEANOR ROOSEVELT

I looked closely at the picture. Among all the women journalists was a familiar face. I was even more amazed to see that familiar face with a hat tilted just so.

"Miss Dobson, what color is the hat you're wearing in this picture?"

She laughed and answered, "Margo, that old gray

hat has traveled many miles with me. I suppose one day I'll get a new one."

"Y-You're E. D. Kirby, the famous writer? And you're the lady with the gray hat who sits in the middle row of the fourth car of the Saturday-night excursion train? All this time, the two people I've always wanted to meet . . . well, they were both my teacher!"

Miss Dobson looked a bit surprised herself, then laughed.

"Margo, Kirby was my mother's maiden name. She always encouraged me to write, so I wanted her name to be a part of my pen name. Her family has owned a newspaper in New York City for many years. That's how my parents met. After my mother passed away, my father decided to retire to a smaller town, where he could publish a newspaper. My uncle pays my fare to and from New York City twice a month. I spend my time interviewing people and writing articles for him. In return, he helps my father. My uncle sends him ink and other equipment to keep the Johnstown paper up and running. It's all very exciting. That's how I met Eleanor Roosevelt. We've known each other for many years as journalists and friends. I knew she was attending a special event in New York City this past weekend. She had asked me to try and meet her there, even though it wasn't one of my regular weekends to travel. Your letter convinced me to go.

I knew I could see her. She'd have received your letter anyway, and she would have answered it. It would have been too late, however. I delivered it for you, and she asked me to give this to you in return."

I slowly opened the envelope Miss Dobson handed me. I wanted to save it because it had the White House as the return address. I pulled out the note inside and Papa's Victory Medal. Once again I read out loud.

*Margo, by now you have received the good news. I would trust only my dear friend E. D. Kirby with this envelope.*

> *Your friend,*
> *Eleanor Roosevelt*

*P.S. I am returning this medal to you and your papa. You have both earned it. It gives President Roosevelt and me great courage to know there are fine young people like you.*

I must have temporarily forgotten where I was and who I was with again. It was the second time I had ever hugged a teacher.

# Chapter 21

## CELEBRATION

The neighbors celebrated with us until late last night. It was funny to think that Maple Avenue was alive with music and laughter because a family was staying where they belonged all along.

Rosa and I sat on the lid of the trunk under my window. I told her the entire story. I would never forget what she said to me. "Margo, you deserve everything good that happens to you. You had the courage to face your problems. Some people choose to ignore them and walk away." It was the only time we ever talked about her father.

When we went back downstairs, Papa was playing his mandolin. Mrs. DiLuso was in the middle of a circle of neighbors dancing the tarantella with Mr. Frappa.

Mrs. Meglio stayed to help Mama after everybody left. It was one the few nights that she wasn't sitting on her front porch waiting for Mr. Meglio to return.

This morning I woke to the sound of Mama's voice. She was still singing. Papa went to the store for a little while, then came home with a basket of pears and fresh farmer's cheese. He told Mama, Charlie, and me to dress warm because he wanted us to go with him.

We took the trolley to the bottom of the Johnstown Inclined Plane. Papa used his pocket change to pay for our cable-car ride to the top of the incline. Charlie and I stood on the deck and looked out over Johnstown. It was exciting. Even in these difficult times, people still went about doing what they had to do. We could see all the different neighborhoods cupped in the valley of the surrounding hills. We found the steel mill and followed the train tracks to Maple Avenue.

We were eating slices of pears and cheese when Papa pointed to the view in front of him.

"Margo and Charlie, this is why your mama and I came to this great country."

I knew we weren't rich with money. Papa never talked about being wealthy. He talked only of being rich in happiness and health, and in always having a good heart that was filled with love. I was proud of Mama and Papa. They had come to this country with a silver ladle, and many dreams.

I knew someday I might have to leave Maple Avenue, but I would always return. No matter where I went, no matter what I did, Johnstown would always be my home.

*The author's grandfather
Mike Coco in his uniform*

# Author's Note

Though *A Letter to Mrs. Roosevelt* is a work of fiction, the heart of the story is true—a letter was written to Mrs. Roosevelt asking for her help, and she did intervene to save my father's home. Storytelling has become a tradition in my family. This book was inspired by a combination of those stories—the heritage of my family.

Johnstown, Pennsylvania, is nestled in a valley of the Allegheny Mountains. It became the home of many immigrants who were willing to work very hard in the steel mills, in the coal mines, on the railroad, and in other businesses. However, the hills that surround Johnstown could not protect these fine people from the black cloud of hunger, desperation, and the loss of work and homes that swept across the United States during the Great Depression.

Grandmother and Grandfather Coco raised five children in their home on Sherman Street. As a proud member of the Yankee Division of the U.S. Army, Grandfather had returned to Johnstown after World War I and named the family-owned business the Yankee Shoe Repair Factory. That business is now in its seventy-eighth year. On New

Year's Day of 1929, my father, who was then just a boy, suffered an injury to his leg. Osteomyelitis, an infection of the bone and bone marrow, set in. Five thousand dollars was needed to call in a doctor from Boston. My grandparents borrowed the money, using everything they owned as collateral. By 1933 the five-thousand-dollar bank loan had become a tremendous burden. The bank threatened to take my grandparents' home.

Grandfather Coco's courage never wavered. He dictated a letter to the First Lady, Eleanor Roosevelt, which my father's older sister, Mary, wrote. She was in the fourth grade. Along with the letter, my grandfather returned his citizenship papers and his induction and honorable discharge papers from the U.S. Army. These papers represented all that my grandfather believed in. If Mrs. Roosevelt could not help him, his letter said, he requested that she keep them, for their true value would be lost. Mrs. Roosevelt intervened, and the valuable papers were returned. It is believed that my grandfather was one of the first in Johnstown to receive a loan through President Roosevelt's Home Owners Loan Corporation (HOLC), which was a part of the New Deal relief program.

I recently read a quote by Martha Gellhorn, a journalist, novelist, and friend of Eleanor Roosevelt. She described the First Lady, on evenings when she had retired to her bedroom after entertaining dinner guests in the White House. She was determined, no matter how busy, to answer her mail. "She sat there until well after midnight, often grey-faced with fatigue, never complaining of this extra duty after a day filled with work. Sometimes I sat with her and read the letters; the most heartbreaking came from young girls, lost in the misery of the Depression. Mrs. R. looked beautiful, the tall woman in the long evening dress, bowed over that cramped desk, concentrated, saddened, her face showing that she heard these voices calling for her help."

I have often wondered if Grandfather Coco's letter, in a young girl's handwriting, lay on that same desk. Though I have exercised artistic liberty in describing many of the landmarks of Johnstown, and my characters are all fictitious, my story is essentially a true one. I hope you will someday visit this city, which has survived desperate times through the sheer courage of its many wonderful citizens. It is the home where my heart will forever be—Johnstown, Pennsylvania.

C. COCO DE YOUNG